277-02 flex 5.

"HELLO READING books are a perfect introduction to reading. Brief sentences full of word repetition and full-color pictures stress visual clues to help a child take the first important steps toward reading. Mastering these story books will build children's reading confidence and give them the enthusiasm to stand on their own in the world of words."

—Bee Cullinan
Past President of the International Reading
Association, Professor in New York University's
Early Childhood and Elementary Education Program

"Readers aren't born, they're made. Desire is planted—planted by parents who work at it."

—Jim Trelease
author of *The Read Aloud Handbook*

"When I was a classroom reading teacher, I recognized the importance of good stories in making children understand that reading is more than just recognizing words. I saw that children who have ready access to story books get excited about reading. They also make noticeably greater gains in reading comprehension. The development of the HELLO READING stories grows out of this experience."

—Harriet Ziefert
M.A.T., New York University School of Education
Author, Language Arts Module,
Scholastic Early Childhood Program

*For A. M. B., who knows
about wishes*

PUFFIN BOOKS
Published by the Penguin Group
Viking Penguin Inc., 40 West 23rd Street, New York, New York 10010, U.S.A.
Penguin Books Ltd, 27 Wrights Lane, London W8 5TZ, England
Penguin Books Australia Ltd, Ringwood, Victoria, Australia
Penguin Books Canada Ltd, 2801 John Street, Markham, Ontario, Canada L3R 1B4
Penguin Books (N.Z.) Ltd, 182-190 Wairau Road, Auckland 10, New Zealand

Penguin Books Ltd, Registered Offices: Harmondsworth, Middlesex, England

First published in Puffin Books, 1989 • Published simultaneously in Canada

1 3 5 7 9 10 8 6 4 2

Text copyright © Harriet Ziefert, 1989
Illustrations copyright © Amy Aitken, 1989
All rights reserved
Library of Congress catalog card number: 88-62145
ISBN 0-14-050981-X

Printed in Singapore for Harriet Ziefert, Inc.

Please Let It Snow

Harriet Ziefert
Pictures by Amy Aitken

PUFFIN BOOKS

I have a new snow suit.

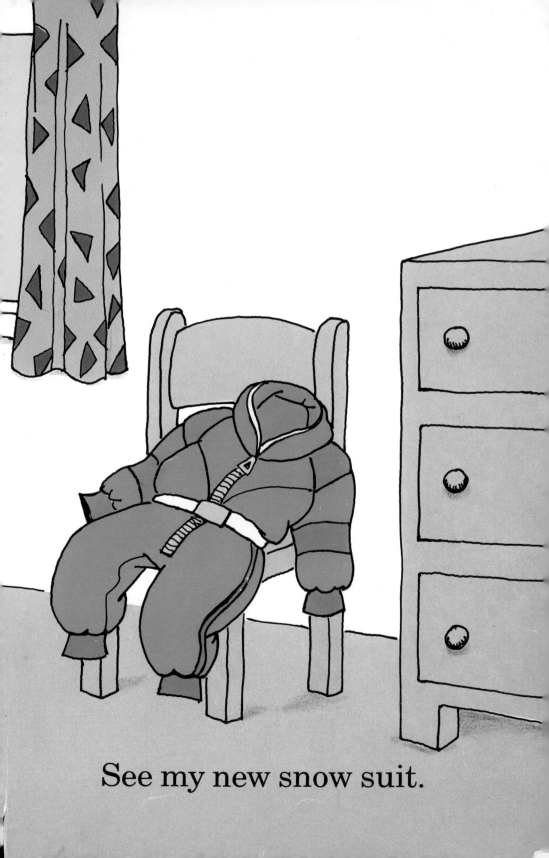

See my new snow suit.

I have a new snow hat.

I have new snow boots.

And I have new mittens.

I wait for snow.

I wait and wait
and wait.
But every day
the sun shines.

In the morning
I run to the window.

I open the shade
and...

the sun is shining!
So I can't wear
my new snow suit.
I can't wear
my new snow hat.

I can't wear
my new snow boots.

And I can't wear
my new mittens.

I get dressed.

But *not* for snow.

Every night I say to myself—
please let it snow...
please let it snow.

But every morning
the sun shines.

I give up!
I stop wishing
for snow.

At night I just
get into bed.

In the morning I do not
even open the shade.

I get dressed.

But *not* for snow.

I walk to the front door
and pull it open.

Guess what?

It snowed!
It *really* snowed!

I put on my new snow suit...

and my new snow hat...

and my new snow boots…

and my new mittens.

See my snow ball!

See my snow angel!

See my snow man!